Duck Derby Debacle

Don't miss a single

# Nancy Drew
# Clue Book:

# Nancy Drew

## * CLUE BOOK *

### #16

## Duck Derby Debacle

BY CAROLYN KEENE * ILLUSTRATED BY PETER FRANCIS

# Aladdin

NEW YORK   LONDON   TORONTO   SYDNEY   NEW DELHI

# ALADDIN

An imprint of Simon & Schuster Children's Publishing Division
1230 Avenue of the Americas, New York, New York 10020
First Aladdin paperback edition July 2021
Text copyright © 2021 by Simon & Schuster, Inc.
Illustrations copyright © 2021 by Peter Francis
Also available in an Aladdin hardcover edition.
ALADDIN and related logo are registered trademarks of Simon & Schuster, Inc.
NANCY DREW, NANCY DREW CLUEBOOK, and colophons
are registered trademarks of Simon & Schuster, Inc.
All rights reserved, including the right of reproduction in whole or in part in any form.
For information about special discounts for bulk purchases, please contact
Simon & Schuster Special Sales at 1-866-506-1949 or business@simonandschuster.com.
The Simon & Schuster Speakers Bureau can bring authors to your live event.
For more information or to book an event contact the Simon & Schuster Speakers Bureau
at 1-866-248-3049 or visit our website at www.simonspeakers.com.
Series designed by Karina Granda
Interior designed by Tom Daly
The illustrations for this book were rendered digitally.
The text of this book was set in Adobe Garamond Pro.
Manufactured in the United States of America 0621 OFF
2 4 6 8 10 9 7 5 3 1
Library of Congress Cataloging-in-Publication Data
Names: Keene, Carolyn, author. | Francis, Peter, illustrator.
Title: Duck Derby debacle / by Carolyn Keene ; illustrated by Peter Francis.
Description: New York : Aladdin, 2021. | Series: Nancy Drew clue book ; 16 | Audience: Ages
6 to 9. | Summary: "The Clue Crew solves a case of missing rubber duckies in the sixteenth
Nancy Drew Clue Book"—Provided by publisher.
Identifiers: LCCN 2020054978 (print) | LCCN 2020054979 (eBook) |
ISBN 9781534450318 (hardcover) | ISBN 9781534450301 (paperback) |
ISBN 9781534450325 (eBook)
Subjects: CYAC: Mystery and detective stories. | Lost and found possessions—Fiction. |
Toy ducks—Fiction.
Classification: LCC PZ7.K23 Duc 2021 (print) | LCC PZ7.K23  (eBook) |
DDC [Fic]—dc23
LC record available at https://lccn.loc.gov/2020054978
LC eBook record available at https://lccn.loc.gov/2020054979

# ∗ CONTENTS ∗

# Duck Derby Debacle

# Chapter

## SIMPLY DUCKY!

"Hundreds of rubber duckies!" Bess Marvin exclaimed. "Can you imagine so many in one place?"

"Or in one bathtub?" George Fayne joked.

Nancy giggled as she and her two best friends walked together, enjoying the summer afternoon. That Friday, the air was as warm as cookies fresh from the oven. It was also full of excitement!

"There'll be lots of room for all those rubber

ducks when they race down the river on Sunday," Nancy said. "And we'll be there to watch!"

The girls couldn't wait until Sunday, but it was already fun-day. There was a pre-derby festival at Mayor Strong's house that afternoon, and it was just for kids!

"How will anyone know whose rubber duck wins the race?" Bess asked. "Most rubber duckies look alike."

"Each rubber duck will have a number, Bess," Nancy explained. "The first to float past the finish line wins."

George gave a thumbs-up as she said, "The owner of the winning duck wins a summer of free movies at the cineplex—popcorn included!"

"Then I'm glad our families have ducks in the race," Bess said. "I just wish kids were allowed to enter too."

"Me too," George said. "Then we'd really be a part of the rubber ducky derby."

Nancy wished they could be more involved as well. There had to be more for them to do than cheer for the racing ducks. Suddenly she had an idea.

"Maybe we can help out at the ducky derby!"

"Help out how?" Bess asked.

"Let's ask Mayor Strong when we get to his house," Nancy said with a smile. "There must be something we can do to be a big part of the event!"

The celebration had already begun when Nancy, Bess, and George arrived at the mayor's mansion. There were tables filled with duck-yellow cupcakes and duck-shaped cookies. There were games, too, like a rubber duck toss. Most of the kids were standing in front of a stage, waiting to watch the River Heights Junior Dancers rock out a number called "Disco Duck."

Nancy, Bess, and George were about to join the crowd when a voice shouted, "There's still time to buy a rubber duck for the derby, plus a chance to win the big prize!"

The voice came from a table set up near the gate. Behind it, a man and two women were selling rubber ducks for five dollars apiece. When they made a sale, the volunteer would toss a duck into a cardboard box. Nancy giggled as each landed with a squeak. The ducks sounded like her puppy Chocolate Chip's squeaky chew toys!

"Remember, everybody!" a woman selling ducks called out. "The money raised will be used to build benches around the River Heights Park duck pond!"

"How many ducks do you think they've sold so far?" Bess asked.

Nancy was about to guess when a voice behind them said, "As of five minutes ago—two hundred eighty ducks."

The girls turned to see Kinsley Armbruster from one of the other third grade classes at school. She wore a bright yellow cap with an orange duck bill and dangly ducky earrings.

"Two hundred eighty ducks, huh?" George said, scrunching her face thoughtfully. "At five dollars apiece . . . that equals one thousand four hundred dollars."

"George won the math bee last week," Nancy said proudly.

"Wow," Kinsley said, clearly impressed. "And I thought the Clue Crew just solved mysteries!"

Nancy, Bess, and George did love solving mysteries—so much so that they called themselves the Clue Crew. They even had a clue book where they wrote down all their clues and suspects.

"Don't you collect rubber duckies, Kinsley?" Nancy asked.

"Yes," Kinsley said, gazing at the table. "But I only have a hundred rubber duckies. I wish I had more."

"More?" George asked. "Aren't a hundred rubber duckies enough?"

"Not if I want to break the record," Kinsley replied.

"What record?" Bess asked.

"The *Kids' World Book of Records*," Kinsley said. "I just need a couple hundred more ducks to break the rubber ducky collection record. Then they'd post my name on their website and I'd be famous!"

"There's still time to collect more," Nancy said.

"Not really," Kinsley sighed. "A judge from the *Kids' World Book of Records* is coming to my house this afternoon to count my ducks."

Bess glanced at her watch. "It's already one thirty. Shouldn't you be home getting ready for the judge's visit?"

Kinsley's duck earrings wiggled as she shook her head. "I want to stay here until three o'clock. They're giving out free T-shirts at the end of the celebration!"

Kinsley gave the girls a little wave, then headed toward the stage to watch the dancers.

"Kinsley loves collecting duck stuff," Bess said. "Maybe I should start collecting something too."

"You already have a huge collection, Bess," George said.

"Of what?" Bess asked.

George looked Bess up and down and said, "Clothes! The judge of the *Kids' World Book of*

*Records* should check out your closet!"

Bess rolled her eyes. She and George were cousins, but they were totally different. Bess had long blond hair and the latest fashion-forward clothes and accessories. Dark-haired George loved clothes too, as long as they were comfy enough to do cartwheels in. She was also an electronics geek—and proud of it!

"There's Mayor Strong," Nancy said with a smile. "Let's ask him about helping out at the ducky derby!"

Mayor Strong turned when he heard Nancy, Bess, and George call his name, beaming as he recognized the city's best young sleuths. "What can I do for you girls?" he asked.

Just as Nancy opened her mouth to reply, a woman stepped between her and the mayor. The girls recognized her at once. It was Dorothy Danner, River Heights's busiest party planner. The Clue Crew knew Dorothy from a missing butterfly case they once worked on. They also knew she could be a drama queen!

"Excuse me, Mayor Strong," Dorothy said briskly. "I need to talk to you at once."

"I was just speaking with the girls, Dorothy," Mayor Strong said. "Can it wait a minute?"

"Not even a second!" Dorothy declared. "This is an emergency!"

Nancy, Bess, and George traded glances. Everything with Dorothy was an emergency.

"I'm planning a baby shower tomorrow morning for Eileen MacDuff," Dorothy explained. "The theme is rubber duckies."

"Mrs. MacDuff?" Nancy asked, grinning. "She's our school librarian."

"Mrs. MacDuff picks out the best books for us to read!" Bess said.

"And she doesn't make us whisper in her library," George added.

Dorothy raised an eyebrow at the girls. "How nice," she said, not smiling, then turned back to the mayor. "Mayor Strong, I'm going to need about a hundred rubber ducks to decorate the table."

"So what's the problem?" Mayor Strong asked.

"My order went to the wrong address," Dorothy wailed. "It's too late to have them redelivered!" She shook her head. "Every store in River Heights donated their ducks to this silly ducky derby!"

Nancy, Bess, and George stared at Dorothy. How could she call the ducky derby silly?

"How can I help, Dorothy?" Mayor Strong asked.

Dorothy pointed to the table just as one of the

volunteers dropped another duck into the box. "Let me buy those rubber duckies for the baby shower."

Mayor Strong shook his head. "Sorry, Dorothy. Those ducks have already been sold. They're racing in the derby on Sunday."

"All of them?" Dorothy cried.

The mayor nodded and said, "I'm afraid you'll have to cook up something else."

Dorothy stared at the mayor for a moment, and then her expression shifted. "Cook up something, huh?" she murmured. "Now, there's an idea."

A suddenly excited Dorothy brushed past the girls. She didn't notice that she bumped George's shoulder as she rushed off.

"Sounds like Dorothy's planning something," Nancy said.

George crossed her arms. "She *is* a party planner, just like my mom, remember?"

"How could we forget?" Bess asked, licking her lips. "Aunt Louise saves us the yummiest leftovers from her parties!"

Mayor Strong glanced toward the stage. "Can your question wait, girls? I have to start up the duck joke contest."

"Sure, Mayor Strong," Nancy said.

George's eyes flashed as the mayor walked away. "Duck joke contest? I know the most awesome duck joke!"

"Tell us, George!" Nancy pleaded.

Bess giggled. "Yes, George! Quack us up!"

"Okay," George said with a grin. "What do you get when you fill a box with ducks?"

Before Nancy and Bess could guess, George blurted out, "A box of quackers! Get it?"

"I got it!" an angry voice snapped. "And I want to get it *back*!"

# Chapter 2

## NO JOKE

Nancy, Bess, and George all groaned at the same time. They would know that voice anywhere.

"Antonio Elefano," Nancy said as the girls turned around.

Antonio stood behind them with his hands on his hips. There were five other kids with him. Each wore red T-shirts that read PROFESSOR CHUCKLE'S COMEDY & CLOWNING CAMP.

"Comedy camp?" Nancy asked.

"Since when are you funny, Antonio?" Bess said.

Antonio shrugged. "Comedy camp wasn't my first choice, but Bug Camp at the zoo was filled up and Camp Daredevil wouldn't dare take me."

"I wonder why," George said under her breath.

"Don't change the subject," he snapped. "You stole my duck joke, and I want it back for the contest . . . *Georgia*!"

"Uh-oh," Bess whispered to Nancy. "George hates when someone uses her real name."

Nancy could see that George was already mad. Her teeth were clenched as she said, "I did not steal your joke, Antonio Elefano, and you know it."

Nancy and Bess exchanged worried looks. What if the showdown between Antonio and

George became too loud? Or nasty? What if they were asked to leave?

"I have an idea!" Nancy said quickly. "Whoever goes first gets to tell the quackers joke. The other person should have another joke ready."

"Fine," George muttered. "I already have another joke, anyway."

"Antonio?" Nancy asked. "Do you have another joke too?"

Antonio looked down as he toed the ground with his sneaker. "Yeah . . . I guess."

"Good," Nancy said, pointing to the stage. "Because it looks like the joke contest is about to start."

The campers began walking toward the stage. Antonio looked over his shoulder and called, "Good luck, George. May the best joke win. . . . *Mine*!" before climbing up the steps.

"Don't worry," Nancy said softly. "Bess and I don't believe Antonio. Of course you didn't steal the quackers joke from him."

"Tell us your other joke," Bess said. "Please?"

"Okay," George said. "Who stole the soap from the bathtub?"

"Who?" Nancy and Bess asked together.

"A robber ducky!" George grinned.

Nancy and Bess doubled over, laughing at George's new joke when—

"Get ready to quack up, because it's time for the duck joke contest!" Mayor Strong boomed into the microphone. "Whoever has a joke, come on up!"

"Me, me, meeeee!" Antonio shouted as he raced to the center of the stage. George took her place behind Antonio and two other kids.

"Antonio is first in line, Nancy," Bess said with a frown. "He'll get to go first and use George's duck joke."

"Okay, kids," Mayor Strong called out. "When I point to you, tell your duck joke in a nice loud voice!"

"*Point* to us?" Antonio cried. "But I was first in line!"

"You'll get your turn, Antonio," Mayor Strong said cheerily. He pointed to George. "Got a joke for us?"

"I do, Mayor Strong!" George said loudly and clearly. "What do you get when you fill a box with ducks . . . ? A box of quackers!"

"A box of quackers!" Mayor Strong guffawed. "Good one!"

Everyone laughed. Everyone except Antonio, whose mouth was a grim line. After two more kids told their jokes, it was his turn.

"Got a joke for us, Antonio?" Mayor Strong asked.

"I did!" Antonio grumbled. "But George told it first!"

The mayor shrugged, then turned to the next jokester, Kendra Jackson. After three more jokes, he introduced Angela Aikens, the winner of the school science fair, to help pick a winner.

Angela smiled as she held up a wiry contraption. "According to my latest laugh-meter invention," she said, "the winner is Kendra

Jackson with her Count Duckula joke!"

Nancy and Bess were happy for Kendra, but disappointed for George. They ran to meet her as she came down from the stage.

"Your joke was really funny, George," Nancy told her.

"You mean *my* joke!" Antonio shouted from a few feet away. "And just for that, the ducky derby is *going down*!"

Nancy wondered what Antonio meant. He'd lost the contest, but why would he take it out on the ducky derby? Nancy didn't have long to think about it. Mayor Strong was trying to quiet the crowd.

She turned her attention back to the stage as the Mayor said, "I was just handed the total number of rubber ducks sold for the derby on Sunday! We've sold three hundred thirty-five rubber duckies—enough to buy *two* benches for the duck pond!"

Loud cheers filled the air.

"We have all our ducks in a row for Sunday,"

Mayor Strong added with a chuckle. "We just need to write your numbers on them before the race."

*Numbers?* The words made Nancy's eyes light up. He had just given her the most awesome idea!

"Bess, George—that's how we can help out! We can write the numbers on the rubber duckies for the race!"

Bess groaned. "All three hundred and thirty-five?"

"Do you think the mayor will let us do it?" George asked.

"There's only one way to find out," Nancy said with a smile. "Let's ask!"

Just as Mayor Strong climbed down from the stage, the girls ran to his side. He listened to Nancy's idea, then asked, "Do you think you can handle this responsibility, girls? Numbering this many ducks is a big job."

"We have lots of waterproof markers in our kitchen drawer," Nancy said. "And my dad can make sure we're doing it right."

Mayor Strong nodded thoughtfully. "I'm sure you'd do a great job. Do you promise to take good care of the ducks and bring them to the riverbank Sunday morning by ten o'clock sharp in time for the race?"

"We promise!" Nancy, Bess, and George replied as one.

"Then congratulations, girls," Mayor Strong declared. "The job is yours!"

The Clue Crew high-fived, then thanked Mayor Strong. They would get to be a big part of the ducky derby on Sunday!

The mayor helped load the box of rubber ducks onto a wagon for the girls to wheel over to Nancy's house. After making sure the box was taped shut, they were on their way.

"Can't we stay a bit longer?" Bess asked as they approached the gate. "Remember what Kinsley said? In less than an hour, they're giving out the free T-shirts!"

Nancy shook her head as she pulled the wagon along the path. "I want to get these ducks

home now," she said. "We have work to do."

They were about to turn onto the street when they heard someone trying to get their attention. "Wait!" Kinsley called.

Nancy stopped wheeling as Kinsley ran to catch up.

"Take a picture of me with all the ducks, please," Kinsley said, waving her phone. "Then I can break the rubber ducky record!"

Nancy, Bess, and George stared silently at Kinsley. Something about her ask just didn't seem right.

"It wouldn't count if they're not your ducks," George said.

"Sorry, Kinsley," Nancy said softly.

Kinsley dropped the hand holding her phone to her side. "No problem. I still have time to find a few hundred ducks before the judge comes later."

The girls watched Kinsley walk back to the festival.

"Where's Kinsley going to find a few hundred ducks in so little time?" Bess wondered.

"She'll think of something," Nancy said. "In the meantime, we have hundreds of ducks to number, so let's get them home."

The girls took turns pulling the wagon. When they reached the Drew house, they worked together to lift the box out of the wagon bed and carefully place it on the doorstep.

"Let's leave the wagon outside while we bring the box of rubber ducks into the house," Nancy suggested.

She was about to open the front door when a familiar tune filled the air. It was the Mr. Drippy ice-cream truck rolling down the street.

"I so want ice cream now!" Bess declared.

"But we have to get the box inside," Nancy said, protesting.

"I could use some ice cream too, Nancy," George admitted. "The box will be safe in your yard."

Nancy looked at the box on the doorstep, then at her friends. "Okay," she said. "But let's be fast, please."

Nancy, Bess, and George found the truck around the corner. Eight-year-old Henderson Murphy was leaning out the window. Henderson

helped his father serve ice cream every summer.

"Name your flavors!" Henderson called with a grin.

"Strawberry, please," Bess said.

"Which strawberry?" Henderson asked. "We have strawberry shortcake, strawberry banana, strawberry kiwi, strawberry—"

"Plain strawberry is fine," Bess said.

"Cup or cone? We have sugar cones, graham cracker cones, gluten-free cones—"

"Henderson, we want speed, not accuracy!" George said. "I'll have one scoop of rocky road in a sugar cone, please."

"I'll have a butter pecan ice-cream cone with chocolate sprinkles," Nancy said before quickly adding, "Please."

"Chocolate sprinkles?" Henderson said. "We have chocolate-mint sprinkles, chocolate cookie sprinkles—"

When he noticed the girls rolling their eyes, he said, "Plain chocolate sprinkles. Got it."

As Henderson scooped ice cream with his

dad, the girls heard a sound louder than the Mr. Drippy tune.

They looked up the street just as a bus turned the corner. Unlike the other buses in River Heights, this one was splashed with bright colors and was honking an old-timey horn!

"Check out that cool bus!" George exclaimed.

"It's the color of rainbow sherbet!" Nancy said.

"Sherbet," Henderson called. "We have lemon, lime . . ."

Once the girls finally got their ice cream, they thanked Henderson and headed back to Nancy's house to get started on their job.

Between licks, Nancy said, "Right after our ice cream break, let's get to work on the rubber ducks."

"Uh . . . what ducks, Nancy?" George asked.

"What do you mean *what ducks*?" Nancy asked. "You know what I'm talking about, George."

"You mean the ducks that were on your doorstep?" George asked.

"*Were?*" Nancy repeated. She looked to see where George was pointing and her jaw dropped. The doorstep was empty! "The box!" Nancy cried. "Bess, George—where's the box of rubber duckies?"

# Chapter 3

## QUACKING THE CASE

Nancy, Bess, and George stared down at the empty doorstep. Then they ran around the outside of the house looking for the box, but the duckies were nowhere to be found.

"Where is it?" Bess cried.

"It couldn't have just disappeared," George insisted.

Nancy took a deep breath, trying to stay calm. "Maybe Hannah saw the box and brought it inside."

Still clutching their ice-cream cones, the girls charged into the house. They found Hannah wheeling a vacuum cleaner into the hall closet. Hannah was the Drews' housekeeper, but had been more like a mother to Nancy since she was three years old.

"Hannah, did you see a big cardboard box

outside on the doorstep about fifteen minutes ago?" Nancy asked.

Chip, Nancy's puppy, scrambled around the girls' feet as they waited for Hannah's answer.

"The only box I know about is that one," Hannah said, pointing.

Nancy turned to see a cardboard box sitting near the door. "What's inside?" she asked.

"Old clothes I'm donating to the March of Time thrift shop," Hannah explained. "The box has been sitting there since this morning."

"Did you hear anything outside, Hannah?" George asked.

"Or someone?" Bess added.

"I did, actually. When I turned off the vacuum cleaner, I heard a car pulling out of the driveway."

"You did?" Nancy asked. "Do you know whose car it was?"

"I didn't look out the window to see," Hannah replied. "I figured it was just making a U-turn. Cars do that around here all the time." Hannah raised an eyebrow. "What's so important about this box?"

Nancy, Bess, and George traded worried looks. If they told Hannah, she might want them to tell Mayor Strong—and they weren't ready to do that.

"We'll let you know, as soon as we find it," Nancy said, forcing a smile.

"Okay," Hannah said. "In the meantime, Chip is finding something yummy on my just-cleaned floor."

Nancy glanced down to see Chip ready to lap at three puddles of melted ice cream!

"Oops!" Nancy said.

"Ice-cream meltdown!" George shouted.

The girls hurried to the kitchen to drop their soggy ice-cream cones in the sink. After wiping up the puddles, they raced to Nancy's

room, trying to control their growing panic.

Nancy groaned. "Hannah said she didn't bring the box inside. Now we know it really is gone."

"We just had to run for the ice-cream truck!" Bess wailed. "What were we thinking?"

"We? *We?*" George shot her cousin a dirty look. "You were the one who wanted ice cream the most!"

"Yes," Bess said, "but who knew Henderson would take so long telling us the million flavors—"

"You guys," Nancy cut in. "What matters most is that we find the rubber duckies."

Bess sighed. "I know, but how could we lose three hundred and thirty-five of them?"

George plopped down on Nancy's bed. "Hannah said she heard a car pulling out of the driveway. If you ask me, those ducks were plucked."

"You mean stolen?" Nancy asked.

"If that's the case, we should tell Mayor Strong!" Bess said.

"Not yet, Bess." Nancy was pacing the room.

"We promised the mayor we'd take good care of the rubber ducks."

"And we goofed." George flopped onto her back. "So what do we do?"

Nancy stopped, placed her hands on her hips, and said, "Let's make our own promise, Clue Crew. We're going to do our best to find the missing ducks!"

"Pinky promise." Bess said, holding up her smallest finger.

"I don't do pinkies," George said, standing up from the bed. "But I do promise."

"I do too," Nancy said. She went to her desk and picked up a pen and their most important tool of all—the Clue Crew's clue book! Then with a smile, she said, "Let's get to work!"

All three girls sat on the floor, leaning against Nancy's bed. Nancy opened the notebook to a clean page and wrote down:

*Who Plucked the Ducks?*

"Let's start with when the box was taken," she said.

"It had to have happened a few minutes before three o'clock," Bess said. "I know because while Henderson was taking forever with our ice cream, I looked at my watch."

Nancy drew a little clock on the page. The hands were pointed close to three o'clock. "We know when the box was taken," she said. "But *who* took the box from the doorstep?"

"Someone who wanted the ducks really badly," George replied. "And knew exactly where to find them."

"Dorothy Danner needed a ton of rubber duckies for Mrs. MacDuff's baby shower tomorrow," Bess said.

"Dorothy drives a catering van," George said. "That could be what Hannah heard pulling out of your driveway."

"Dorothy might have seen us leave the festival with the rubber duckies and followed us all the way here," Bess suggested.

"We know she would do *anything* for a perfect party," George said. "And now she's the perfect suspect."

"Our *first* suspect." Nancy started her suspect list and added Dorothy Danner to the top of it. "Who else would want a whole box of rubber duckies?"

Bess grabbed a stuffed unicorn from Nancy's bed and bounced it on her lap. "Antonio said George stole his duck joke. Maybe he and his campmates stole the box to get even."

"We heard Antonio say the ducky derby was

going down," George said. "And if we don't find those ducks, he'll be right."

Nancy was about to add Antonio's name to the list when she remembered the wagon in the yard. "The box of rubber ducks was taken, but the wagon we wheeled it in was left in my yard."

"So?" George asked.

"So the box was heavy," Nancy explained. "Antonio and the campers would have needed the wagon to wheel it back to camp."

"Unless their camp isn't very far," Bess said. "Where is Professor Chuckle's Comedy and Clown Camp, anyway?"

"I'll look it up," George said, happy to have an excuse to use Nancy's computer.

Nancy and Bess watched over George's shoulders as she opened up the camp website. The colorful page showed kids wearing clown noses and big smiles. In one image, a girl stood onstage behind a mike. In another picture, a boy wearing a funny hat juggled rubber chickens.

"It says the camp is held every summer inside Giggles Comedy Club on Blossom Street," George pointed out.

"I think Blossom Street is around the corner from Main Street," Nancy said. "See if there's a map."

George scrolled down the page. There was map—and something else!

"You guys," George said slowly. "Do you see what I see?"

Nancy leaned over George's shoulder to stare at the screen. "I sure do!" she said excitedly. "It looks like Antonio's camp has their own bus!"

"A rainbow-sherbet-colored bus," Bess added, "with an old-timey horn!"

# Chapter

4

## HIDE-AND-SQUEAK

"That's the one!" George said, pointing to the screen. "That's the bus that drove past the ice-cream truck!"

"It sure looks like it," Bess agreed. "But what does it have to do with the missing ducks?"

"The bus was probably taking the campers back to camp from the celebration at the mayor's mansion," Nancy said.

George turned around to face the others. "And remember, the bus came from around the corner, which means it drove past your house, Nancy."

Nancy had an excited gleam in her eye. "If Antonio was on the bus, he might have seen the box from the window. Maybe he asked the driver to stop so he could get off and take it!"

"Would the bus driver have done that?" Bess asked.

"I'm not sure," Nancy said. "But I am sure of something else."

"What?" George asked.

Nancy grinned at her friends. "We have to go duck-hunting at Professor Chuckle's Comedy and Clowning Camp!"

Nancy, Bess, and George raced down the stairs, said goodbye to Hannah, and headed toward Main Street.

They'd all agreed to the same rule with their parents: they could walk anywhere without an adult as long as it was within five blocks of home and they were together. Together was more fun anyway!

The girls were about to turn the corner onto Blossom Street when—

"Oh, Nancy, Bess, George!" a voice called.

The girls froze. Mayor Strong! He was waving as he walked over.

"Oh no!" Bess whispered. "What if Mayor Strong asks us about the rubber ducks?"

"We duck the question, that's what!" George hissed.

"Uh . . . hi, Mayor Strong!" Nancy blurted out.

"Just the girls I want to see!" Mayor Strong said. "I'd like to send a photographer to your house tomorrow, Nancy."

"A photographer?" Nancy asked. "To do what, Mayor Strong?"

"To take pictures of you girls numbering the rubber ducks, of course!" He smiled. "I'd like to post the pictures on the ducky derby website before the race on Sunday."

Nancy, Bess, and George were too stunned to speak. What if they couldn't find the ducks before tomorrow morning? What would they tell Mayor Strong?

"Wouldn't that be fun?" Mayor Strong asked. "I'll have someone from my office contact your parents for permission—"

"Parents?" Nancy cut in. She didn't want her dad to find out about the missing ducks either. At least, not until they were all found!

"Is that okay with you?" Mayor Strong asked.

"No!" George shouted.

"Why not?" Mayor Strong asked, taking a step back.

"Because . . . because Bess is totally camera shy!" George said. "She hates having her picture taken."

"George!" Bess whispered. "I love having my picture taken—"

"Also, umm . . ." Nancy said. "The way we number our ducks is top secret."

"Top secret?" Mayor Strong asked, sounding surprised.

"We're detectives," Nancy explained. "Everything the Clue Crew does is top secret."

Nancy and her friends stood frozen, waiting for the mayor to reply.

"All right then," he finally said. "Why don't you girls think about it and let me know?"

He began to walk away, but glanced back over his shoulder, looking confused.

"He can tell something's wrong," Bess whispered.

"But he doesn't know what yet," George hissed back.

Nancy took a deep breath. They didn't have time to argue. "Let's find those rubber duckies before anyone *finds out*!"

Nancy, Bess, and George hurried up Blossom Street to an old brick building with a sign in the window that read GIGGLES COMEDY CLUB. The only vehicle in the small parking lot was the rainbow-sherbet-colored bus.

"Could the box be inside the bus?" Bess asked.

Nancy shook her head. "If Antonio and his friends did take the box, they probably carried it inside."

"Then what are we waiting for?" George said. "Let's go inside too!"

The girls stepped up to the front door. George twisted the doorknob and it swung open.

"It's not locked," George said, "Are we lucky or what?"

"Lucky ducks!" Bess giggled.

Nancy, Bess, and George filed through the door into the comedy club. The lobby was quiet and empty. All four walls were painted dark red and covered with autographed pictures. A ticket counter stood against one wall.

"What are the people in the pictures famous for?" Bess asked.

"Probably for being funny," George said. "But where are the campers?"

"Shh," Nancy whispered. She nodded at a gold-colored curtain next to the counter. "I hear voices behind there."

The girls peeked through the curtain's panels into a room filled with small tables and chairs.

"That must be the comedy club," Nancy whispered.

George grinned. "And in the back, that must be the comedy camp!"

Nancy looked past the tables and chairs. Antonio and his campmates were standing on a stage. Some wore red clown noses. Some wore funny hats. All of them were around a table, holding cans.

"What are they doing?" George whispered.

"They're squirting something into pans," Nancy whispered. "It looks like whipped cream."

"Comedy, clowning, *and* cooking?" Bess whispered. "This camp has everything!"

A man wearing a red clown nose and giant bow tie around his neck stood near the campers, giving them instructions.

"That's Professor Chuckle," George whispered. "I saw his picture on the website."

Nancy leaned forward a little more. "I'm glad he's keeping the campers busy so we can look for the missing box."

"Look where?" Bess asked.

Nancy didn't know where to start. But then she spotted something a few feet away.

"Over there! A cardboard box!" Nancy pointed through the curtain. "It's the same size as the box the duckies were in!"

"I see it too!" Bess whispered.

"We have to look inside," George added. "See if it's filled with rubber ducks."

"Yeah, but how do we do that without the campers or Professor Chuckle seeing us?" Nancy asked.

"No problem," George whispered. "If we crawl across the floor, the tables and chairs will hide us from view."

"But we'll get our knees all dirty," Bess whispered.

George glared at her.

"Oh, okay."

The Clue Crew dropped to their hands and knees. With George leading the way, they crawled toward the box.

"It's taped shut," Bess whispered. "If we pull the tape off, it'll make a loud noise. The campers will hear us."

"There's a narrow space between the flaps," Nancy said. "One of us can squeeze our hand in and feel for rubber ducks."

"Bess, your hands are the smallest," George whispered. "Go for it!"

Bess slipped her hand through the crack. After digging around, she said, "I feel something . . . but it doesn't feel like a rubber ducky."

"Well, what does it feel like?" Nancy whispered.

"Like something round. And—"

*SQUEEEEEEAK!*

The girls froze. They hoped the campers hadn't heard.

Their hopes were dashed when Antonio's voice sneered, "Come out, come out, wherever you are!"

"Great," George grumbled.

The girls slowly stood. The campers and Professor Chuckle were staring straight at them.

"Uh . . . hi!" Nancy said with a small wave.

No one said hi back. Instead, Antonio and the other campers lifted their pie pans and charged toward Nancy, Bess, and George!

"Ready?" Antonio shouted. "Aim . . . hurl!"

# Chapter

5

## YELL PHONE

The Clue Crew covered their faces as they braced for a shower of pie cream. Instead, a deep voice shouted, "STOP!"

Peeking between her fingers, Nancy saw Professor Chuckle shaking his head as he made his way toward the campers. "Wrong, kids. Wrong! That's not the way clowns and comedians use cream pies."

The kids lowered their pies.

"A pie in the face is supposed to be funny,"

Professor Chuckle explained. "Not scary."

"And that was not funny!" Bess scolded.

Antonio turned to Professor Chuckle. "Sorry. It's just that those girls are spying on our camp."

"What makes you think they're spying?" Professor Chuckle asked.

"They go to our school," a girl wearing a camp T-shirt said. "They're detectives, so they're always spying on someone."

A boy wearing a clown nose added, "I think they call themselves the Clue Zoo."

"That's Clue *Crew*!" George said.

"And we *are* detectives, Professor Chuckle," Nancy said. "Except we weren't spying."

"We were looking for something," Bess explained.

George was still glaring at the campers. "Something snatched from Nancy's doorstep."

Professor Chuckle adjusted his bow tie. "Unless you tell us what you're looking for, we can't help you find it."

Nancy, Bess, and George traded worried looks.

If they admitted the rubber ducks were missing, Antonio and the others might tell Mayor Strong!

"We were looking for squeaky things," Nancy said. "Like what's in that cardboard box."

"Squeaky like this?" Professor Chuckle asked. He reached up to squeeze the clown nose he wore. It made a loud squeak just like the squeak that had come from the box.

"*That's* what's in the box?" Nancy asked. "Clown noses?"

Professor Chuckle smiled as he yanked off the tape, reached inside, and pulled out a handful of round red rubber clown noses. "You can never have too many clown noses," he said. "You'd be surprised how many get sneezed off."

Nancy glanced inside the box and saw oodles of clown noses. "Thanks, Professor Chuckle," she said.

"Now *I'd* like to know something." Antonio said angrily. "What made you think we took a box off your doorstep?"

"Because you were mad at George for her

duck joke," Nancy explained. "Your camp bus drove past my house at about three o'clock today, around the same time as when the box went missing."

"Someone could have seen the box from their bus window and decided to take it," Bess added.

"I don't think so," Professor Chuckle said. "The campers were too excited to be gazing out the bus windows today."

"Excited about what?" Nancy asked.

Professor Chuckle turned to the campers. "Show them, kids!"

The campers reached into their pockets and pulled out tickets. Each one had a number on it.

"I bought six rubber ducks for the derby on Sunday," Professor Chuckle explained. "One duck for each camper."

"So we all have a duck in the race," Antonio explained. "Whoever wins gets free movies and popcorn for all of us!"

The other campers cheered.

While the campers chatted about how fun the

rest of their summer was going to be when one of them won, the girls regrouped.

"The campers didn't take the box," Nancy said.

"I don't think so either," George replied. "Why would they want to ruin the derby if they each had a chance to win?"

But Bess still wasn't convinced. "Antonio told us that the ducky derby was going down!" she insisted. Her voice was loud enough for everyone to hear—including Antonio!

"What I said about the ducky derby was a joke!" Antonio explained. "Duck feathers are called *down*. Down . . . down . . . get it?"

"I get it!" Professor Chuckle guffawed. "And for that ducktacular joke, Antonio wins the day's golden chicken!"

Antonio puffed his chest out proudly as Professor Chuckle handed him a chicken-shaped trophy.

"I believe Antonio now, Nancy," Bess said. "He's clean."

"No, he's not!" George said. "Look!"

Nancy and Bess turned and gasped. Antonio's face was dripping with pie cream!

"Did I do it right, Professor Chuckle?" the girl wearing the camp T-shirt asked.

"Absolutely, Julia!" Professor Chuckle replied.

"When it comes to a pie in the face—surprise is everything!"

"So is taste," Antonio said as he licked the cream around his mouth. "Yum-o!"

Nancy, Bess, and George were leaving the theater when Professor Chuckle called out, "Wait! You never told us what was inside the missing box!"

"Can't, Professor Chuckle," Nancy replied. "Detectives have surprises too, you know."

The girls left the building and walked to Main Street. Once they got to the corner, Nancy opened their clue book.

"Antonio is no longer a suspect," Nancy said, crossing his name off the list, "So we have just one suspect left."

"Dorothy Danner!" Bess stated.

George glanced down at her black-and-purple sports watch. "It's four o'clock. I promised my mom I'd be home before dinner to play with my little brother—"

"Dorothy Danner! Dorothy Danner!" Bess exclaimed.

George rolled her eyes. "We heard you the first time, Bess!"

"We know Dorothy is our only suspect," Nancy added.

"No!" Bess said lowering her voice. "I mean Dorothy Danner is right there. Look!"

Sure enough, Nancy saw Dorothy leaning against her van and talking on her cell phone.

"I wonder who she's talking to," Nancy said.

"Let's go over and listen," George suggested.

"Isn't that snooping?" Bess asked.

"Not when she's talking so loudly!" George said.

While Dorothy was looking the other way, the girls scrambled behind a big tree near the van. From there, they could hear every word Dorothy was saying.

"You'll have the rubber duckies at your shower tomorrow, Eileen," Dorothy promised. "Enough to decorate all of the tables!"

Nancy felt Bess squeeze her arm. Dorothy had gotten the rubber ducks she wanted!

"You want to know how I got them?" Dorothy continued. "Well, let's just say I thought outside the box."

Nancy stared at Bess and George. "Did Dorothy just say *box*? As in the missing box of rubber duckies?"

# Chapter 6

## SWEET-AND-SHOWER

The girls huddled close against the tree to hear more. Dorothy's voice carried loud and clear.

"I'll see you at ten o'clock at your baby shower tomorrow, Eileen," she said into her phone. "In the meantime, I've got a ton of work to do tonight."

Nancy, Bess, and George peeked out to watch Dorothy climb into her van before she started it and drove up Main Street.

"We have to go to Mrs. MacDuff's baby

shower tomorrow," Nancy said as they hurried out from behind the tree. "Then we'll be able to see those rubber ducks with our own eyes."

"But we weren't invited," George protested.

"Mrs. MacDuff *is* our school librarian," Nancy explained. "We can pretend we're dropping by to say congratulations."

"Drop by where?" Bess asked. "We don't know where Mrs. MacDuff lives."

"She lives on Poppy Street," George said confidently. "My mom and I went to her yard sale last spring."

"Poppy Street is just four blocks away from my house," Nancy said. "We can all walk to the baby shower together." Then she wrote the name of the street in her clue book. "Meet me at my house tomorrow morning at ten o'clock. That's the time Dorothy said she'd be getting to the party."

Bess gave a little excited hop. "We're going to a baby shower! I'm going to wear my new green sundress and white sandals."

"I'll wear a dress too," Nancy said. "What are you going to wear, George?"

She shrugged. "I'll think of something."

Bess frowned, glancing down at George's holey sneakers. "That's what I'm afraid of."

"How would you like your burger, Nancy?" Mr. Drew called from the grill.

"With cheese, please, Daddy," Nancy called back as she set the table in the backyard. "Two slices!"

"One cheesy cheeseburger, coming up!"

Nancy smiled as she set a caddy of forks on the picnic table. Friday nights in the summer were barbecue nights at the Drew house. Mr. Drew loved flipping burgers, veggie kabobs, and ribs while wearing one of his funny aprons. Tonight he was wearing one that read WHO INVITED ALL THESE HUNGRY PEOPLE?

"By the way, where did the wagon in the front yard come from?" Mr. Drew asked above the sizzling noise.

*Wagon?* Nancy's eyes widened. How could she explain the wagon to her father without having to explain the rubber ducks?

"Um . . . Someone lent it to me. I'm going to use it to give Chip rides around the block."

"Rides, huh?" Mr. Drew shrugged. "Okay."

Nancy laid out three paper plates on the table. Over her shoulder, she called, "Daddy? Did you see a big cardboard box around?"

"The only box I've seen is the one of old clothes we're donating." He placed cheese slices on Nancy's burger. "Why?"

Nancy's hands froze above the table, holding a napkin. She'd been counting on not having to explain. Thinking fast, she said, "I was hoping for an early birthday present. Or a late one!"

"Is everything okay, Nancy?" Mr. Drew asked.

"Yes, Daddy!" Nancy answered quickly. "As Hannah would say, a-okay."

"Good," Mr. Drew said, peeking around the grill to give Nancy a nod. "You do know you can come to me with any problem, big or small, right?"

"I know," Nancy said, placing the last napkin on the table. "I'll go inside and see if Hannah needs help with the salad."

Nancy could feel her father watching her as she darted into the house. Shutting the door behind her, she closed her eyes and took a deep breath.

"How long?" Nancy murmured to herself. "How long can I keep this secret?"

Suddenly—

*SQUEAK, SQUEAK, SQUEAK!*

Nancy's eyes popped open. The rubber ducks were squeaky! But where in the house could they be? How?

Nancy followed the squeaks through the house until she found Chocolate Chip in the kitchen chewing on a bone-shaped toy—that squeaked.

"If only you could talk, Chip," Nancy sighed. "Then maybe you could tell me who took the rubber duckies."

Nancy tried not to think or talk about rubber duckies as she enjoyed her cheeseburger. Later that night, she fell asleep hoping the ducks at the baby shower would be the missing ones.

When she woke up early the next morning, she was determined to find out. . . .

"Thanks for being right on time," Nancy told Bess and George as they walked to Mrs. MacDuff's house. "Now we can get to the shower while it's just getting started."

"How can I *not* be on time with the new cuckoo clock my mom put in our kitchen?" George groaned.

"Cuckoo clock?" Nancy asked.

George nodded. "Every hour, a tiny mechanical bird pops out of the clock, chirping, 'Cuckoo. Cuckoo,' really loudly!"

"That's enough to make anyone cuckoo!" Bess giggled.

When the Clue Crew reached the MacDuff house, they saw Dorothy Danner's van parked down the street. The girls walked to the front door, but heard voices coming from around the corner.

"Listen," George said. "It sounds like the baby shower's in the backyard."

Nancy, Bess, and George walked through the yard to investigate.

Duck-shaped balloons fluttered in the breeze. Tables were draped with duck-printed tablecloths and filled with platters of duck-shaped cookies.

The party was already in full swing. Toward the back of the yard sat Mrs. MacDuff opening presents. As she pulled a tiny baby sweater from a gift bag, her guests *ooh*ed and *aah*ed.

"This is so cute!" Mrs. MacDuff exclaimed. "And the little booties that match—*super* cute!"

"Sooooo cute!" other guests chorused.

"Hey, I have a fun idea," George whispered. "Every time they say the word *cute*, let's eat a cookie!"

"We have no time for games, George," Nancy whispered. "Look around the yard for rubber duckies!"

It didn't take long for the girls to find them. Nancy pointed to a nearby table. Scattered all over it were the bright yellow rubber duckies they needed to get back!

"Are we sure those are the real deal?" George whispered.

Bess crossed her arms. "If they look like a duck, and squeak like a duck—"

"We should get a closer look," Nancy cut in.

Mrs. MacDuff and her guests were too busy admiring baby presents to see the girls racing toward the table. George picked up one of the ducks between her thumb and index finger. "I wonder if this one passes the squeak test," she said.

"Don't squeeze it, George!" Nancy said. "If the duck squeaks, Mrs. MacDuff and her guests will turn around!"

As Nancy reached for the duck, she accidentally knocked it from George's hand. It dropped to the ground with a *SPLAT*!

The girls stared down at the dropped ducky. The fall had practically flattened it!

"If the ducky is rubber, why didn't it bounce or roll?" Nancy asked slowly.

"Let's try another one," Bess said before grabbing another duck and dropping it. Just like the first, it fell with a *splat*, sticking to the ground. But that wasn't all . . .

"*Ewww!*" Bess said, pointing to the ground. "Look at that army of ants marching toward the mess!"

Nancy stared down at the hungry ants. "Ants? These ducks are definitely not rubber."

George lifted one of the ducks off the ground before the ants could get to it. She squeezed it between her fingers. It squished even more. "You're right, Nancy. These ducks aren't made out of rubber. They're—"

"Can I help you girls?" someone said.

The girls whirled around. Standing a few feet away with her hands on her hips was—

"Dorothy!" Nancy said quickly. "I mean . . . Ms. Danner!"

# Chapter 7

## GET THE SCOOP

Dorothy tapped her chin as she studied Nancy, Bess, and George. "You were the girls at the mayor's house yesterday," she said. "How do you know Eileen?"

"Mrs. MacDuff is our school librarian, remember?" Nancy responded.

"But we're not here to borrow books," George said. "We're investigating if the ducks on the tables are the same as the ones in the race tomorrow."

Dorothy wrinkled her nose. "You mean the ducky derby? The ducks racing tomorrow are rubber!"

"And these are not," Nancy replied. She pointed to the ground. "The hungry ants mean those ducks are meant to be eaten, not floated."

Dorothy smiled. "The ducks on the tables *can* be eaten, and they're delicious. Who wants to try a fresh one?"

"Sure," Bess said. "Why should ants have all the fun?"

Dorothy took three ducks from the table. She handed one to each girl. George was the first to take a bite.

"How does it taste?" Nancy asked.

"Familiar!" George said between nibbles. "These ducks are made of a candy called *marzipan*."

"Mar-zi-pan?" Nancy repeated carefully.

George nodded. "My mom sometimes makes marzipan for parties she caters."

"Your mom is a caterer too?" Dorothy asked. "Could her name be Louise Fayne?"

"Yes. Do you know my mom?" George responded.

"Who do you think helped me make these candy ducks?" Dorothy asked with a smile. "When I couldn't get enough rubber ducks, I had the brilliant idea for *edible* ducks."

Dorothy pointed at the table. "I wanted them made of marzipan so they could be molded to look like rubber duckies."

"No wonder they're squishy!" Nancy declared.

"And yummy!" Bess added.

"I knew Louise had a fabulous recipe," Dorothy went on. "I went to her house yesterday to get it from her."

Dorothy turned away from the girls to check out the festivities. While she was occupied, Nancy whispered, "How do we know all the ducks are made of candy? Dorothy could still have taken our rubber ones."

"I know how," George whispered. "Watch." George gently tapped on Dorothy's elbow. "Ms.

Danner? What time were you at my house yesterday?"

"It was just before three o'clock," Dorothy said. "Your mom and I compared recipes in the kitchen until about four."

"While you were there, did you notice a clock?" George asked.

Dorothy groaned. "How could I miss it? Your mom has the loudest cuckoo clock I've ever heard!"

"Bingo!" George grinned, pumping her fist in the air.

"Bingo?" Dorothy gasped. "How could I forget to put out the Baby-Name-Bingo cards? Pardon me, girls!"

Nancy, Bess, and George watched as Dorothy hurried off.

"If Dorothy knew about the cuckoo clock, then she told the truth about being at your house yesterday," Nancy said.

George nodded. "We saw Dorothy at four yesterday. She already knew she'd have the candy ducks, so she must have been with my mom around three."

"Your mom—and the cuckoo clock!" Nancy giggled.

"That's not just a cuckoo clock, George," Bess chuckled. "It's a *clue-clue* clock!"

"And the ducks on the tables are not the missing ones," Nancy concluded. She pulled out the clue book from a pocket in her dress and crossed Dorothy's name off the suspect list. When she was done, she said, "Let's pick up the other duck we dropped."

"I'll pick up the duck," Bess said, making a face. "*After* you shoo away the ants!"

Mrs. MacDuff was still busy opening presents as the Clue Crew left.

"We have no more suspects," Nancy sighed as they walked down the street. "Zero, zip, zilch."

"What do we do now?" George asked.

"I know!" Bess said as the Mr. Drippy truck rolled slowly by. "We get ice cream!"

"Your sweet tooth must be super sweet, Bess," Nancy said. "We just ate marzipan duckies."

"And we bought ice cream yesterday," George said. "That's what got us in this mess."

"The ice cream melted yesterday and made a mess," Bess argued. "I demand a do-over."

The truck stopped in the middle of the block. Henderson popped his head out and greeted the girls.

"Hi, Henderson," Bess said as they approached the window. "I'll have a coconut chocolate chip cone, please."

Henderson shouted toward the back of the truck: "Daaad? Is coconut chocolate chip the flavor we ran out of?"

"That's the one, Henderson," Mr. Murphy shouted back. "That girl, Kinsley Armbruster, cleaned us out!"

*Kinsley Armbruster?* Before Nancy could say anything, Henderson popped his head back out the window.

"Like I thought, we're out of coconut chocolate

chip. Sorry. We still have coconut cherry, coconut almond fudge, coconut rocky road—"

"Excuse me, Henderson," Nancy interrupted. "What did your dad mean when he said Kinsley cleaned you out?"

"Does it mean she bought the last of the coconut chocolate chip?" Bess asked.

"Correct!" Henderson said. "Kinsley wanted a cone with three scoops."

"That's not an ice cream cone," George said. "It's an ice cream skyscraper!"

Henderson shrugged. "Kinsley was in a great mood. She wanted to celebrate with a big cone of her favorite flavor."

"What was she celebrating?" Nancy asked.

"Something to do with ducks," Henderson replied. "Some record she broke."

Nancy, Bess, and George gaped at Henderson, then looked at one another.

Did he just say . . . *ducks*? And *record*?

# Chapter

8

## QUACK-IN-THE-BOX

"What duck record, Henderson?" Nancy asked eagerly.

"You have to tell us!" George urged.

"Please?" Bess begged.

"I don't know," Henderson insisted. "She didn't say!"

"Girls?" Mr. Henderson called from inside the truck. "Do you want ice cream or not?"

"Yes, Mr. Drippy—I mean Mr. Murphy!" Nancy replied. "But first we have work to do."

Bess sighed as the girls stepped away from the truck. "We'll never get ice cream!" she grumbled.

"This is bigger than ice cream, Bess!" George said. "Somehow, Kinsley found a couple of hundred rubber ducks to break the record!"

"Maybe the ducks are the missing ones," Nancy said. "We have to go to Kinsley's house and see them for ourselves."

"Does anyone know where Kinsley lives?" Bess asked.

"I do!" Henderson called. "We were parked outside her house on Berry Lane."

"Thanks, Henderson!" Nancy said.

"No problem. You know, we have berry flavors too. Strawberry, blueberry, loganberry—"

Henderson's voice trailed off as the girls hurried away. Nancy opened her clue book to add a new suspect: Kinsley Armbruster! "The ducky derby is tomorrow," she said. "If we're going to question Kinsley, we have to do it right now!"

"Berry Lane is two blocks away," Bess said.

"Then let's hurry to the Berry!" George declared.

When the girls reached Berry Lane, they found several colorful houses.

"Which one is Kinsley's?" Nancy asked.

"Wild guess: the bright yellow one with the duck on the mailbox?" George said.

Nancy narrowed her eyes at the duck. "It's a good guess. The name on the mailbox is Armbruster."

"That's us!" a friendly voice called.

The girls turned to see a woman walking from the house down the path toward them.

"I'm Kinsley's mom," Mrs. Armbruster said. "You girls must be here to see her."

"Yes, please," Bess replied.

"Why don't you go upstairs to Kinsley's room while I get the mail? I'm sure she can't wait to tell you the great news."

George smiled. "We can't wait to hear it."

"Thanks, Mrs. Armbruster!" Nancy said quickly.

The Clue Crew went through the front door and up the stairs. On the second landing, they saw a door decorated with duck stickers.

"This must be the place," George said.

Nancy knocked three times, but there was no answer. She called Kinsley's name through the door. Still no answer.

"She could be listening to music," George suggested. "Let me try."

George gave the door two hard knocks. On the third knock, it popped open.

"Kinsley?" Bess called as they peeked around the door.

Kinsley wasn't in her room, but as Nancy, Bess, and George stepped inside, they saw it was far from empty. Floor-to-ceiling everything was ducky!

"Duck curtains!" Nancy said.

"A duck-shaped lamp," Bess exclaimed. "And look, duck wallpaper!"

"She even has duck slippers," George said, nodding at a pair of plush yellow duckies sitting next to Kinsley's bed. "You don't see those every day."

Nancy walked over to a bookcase against one wall. While the bottom shelf was filled with books, the other shelves were filled with—"Rubber duckies!" Nancy gasped. She waved Bess and George over.

Some of the ducks looked like rock stars or superheroes, but most were yellow with smiling orange beaks—just like the missing ones!

"Guys, Kinsley needed a couple hundred more ducks to break the record," Nancy said.

"Are you saying we have to count all those ducks?" Bess asked, her eyes going wide. "Do we have to squeeze them too?"

"What do you think, George?" Nancy asked. "How many rubber ducks would you say are on these shelves?"

George didn't answer. When Nancy turned around, George was standing over Kinsley's desk.

"Check out her laptop," George said. "Sweet!"

"Don't touch it, George," Nancy called.

"I just touched the mouse, and look," George said, pointing at the screen. "Kinsley had left open the website for the *Kids' Book of World Records*. There's an article here about a girl who broke the rubber ducky record."

"Was it Kinsley?" Nancy asked.

George shook her head. "No, according to this, the girl's named Ruby Rodriquez."

Nancy, Bess, and George all leaned in to see a

picture of Ruby surrounded by hundreds of rubber duckies. *Seven hundred!*

"I don't get it," Bess said. "Kinsley told Henderson she broke the rubber ducky record."

"Maybe Kinsley came in second," Nancy said. "Scroll down. See if they mention her."

George was about to when Bess called, "Omigosh! You guys, look there!"

Nancy and George followed Bess's gaze to the corner of the room. Sitting on the floor was a big cardboard box!

"That looks like the box we left on your doorstep, Nancy," Bess said excitedly. "The one that's missing!"

"Maybe it's not missing anymore!" Nancy said, excited.

She and George rushed to join Bess. Like the missing box, the top was taped closed, but sticking out through the flaps was a brown string.

"What do you think this is for?" George asked after she'd loosened the tape. She took hold of the string and gave it a tug.

*POOOOOOOOOOOOOFFFFFFF!!!!*

The top of the box burst open. Nancy, Bess, and George shrieked as a yellow duck began oozing out, then kept growing and growing.

"That's not a rubber ducky!" Nancy cried.

"It's Duck-zilla!" George shouted. "Run!"

# Chapter

9

## MIX-UP FIX-UP

Nancy, Bess, and George raced to the door just as Kinsley was returning. She looked past the girls and called out, "Holy ravioli!" She pushed her way inside. "I go to the bathroom for a few minutes and come back to find you Clue Snoops going through my things?"

The duck made a loud hiss before it finally stopped growing.

"Your things? As in your giant attack duck?" George asked, trying to calm her breathing.

"It's a giant self-inflatable duck *raft*!" Kinsley insisted.

"Raft?" Nancy repeated.

Kinsley nodded. "I tried to break the record for having the biggest duck raft," she explained, "but a kid named Percy had one twice as big."

"Wow," Bess said.

"We thought you wanted to break the record for having the most rubber ducks," George said, pointing to the computer. "The site says a girl named Ruby beat you to it."

"That's okay," Kinsley said as she walked to her desk. "I broke another record and it's just as awesome."

The ginormous duck raft practically filled the room, pressing up against the girls. Kinsley squeezed her way around it and walked to her desk. She grabbed her laptop and brought it over to show the Clue Crew, pointing to a new page on the *Kids' Book of World Records* site. "I broke the record for the most tries to break a record!"

"They have a record for that too?" Nancy asked.

"Congrats, Kinsley," George said. "But that doesn't mean you weren't still trying to break the rubber ducky record."

"With, say, a couple of hundred ducks you suddenly acquired out of nowhere," Bess added.

Kinsley scrunched her nose. "What are you talking about?" she asked.

Nancy was still reluctant to let anyone know the duckies had gone missing until they found them. "Kinsley, I have question for you. Where were you yesterday at three o'clock?"

"Three o'clock in the afternoon?" Kinsley asked. "I must have still been at the celebration at the mayor's house."

"Are you sure?" Bess asked.

"I stayed until the very end, and that was three o'clock."

While Kinsley focused on releasing the air from the raft, George whispered, "How do we know Kinsley's telling the truth?"

"Yeah," Bess said. "How can we be sure she

was at the mayor's house yesterday until the festival ended?"

Nancy didn't have an answer—until she spotted something bright yellow spread on Kinsley's bed. It was a T-shirt from the mayor's ducky derby celebration.

Pointing to the T-shirt, Nancy said, "Guys, Kinsley did stay at the mayor's house until three o'clock. That's when they were going to give out those T-shirts."

"Hel-lo?" Kinsley called above the hissing raft.

"I'm right here, and I can hear every word you're saying, Clue Crew!"

"We were just working on a case," Nancy admitted with a sheepish smile. "Thanks for helping us figure it out, Kinsley."

"Sure," Kinsley said. "And now you guys can help me."

"How?" Nancy asked.

"Help me get the air out of this humongous duck raft!" Kinsley groaned. "It's taking forever."

"Don't worry, Kinsley," George said, bending her arm to flex her muscle. "Duck-zilla is about to meet his match!"

Nancy, Bess, and George laughed along with Kinsley as they all worked together to squeeze air out of the raft. When Duck-zilla was as flat as a pancake, the girls rolled it neatly and put it back into the box.

"Thanks, Clue Crew," Kinsley said, walking the girls out of the house. "See you at the ducky derby tomorrow."

*Ducky derby!* Nancy gulped. They were having

so much fun in Kinsley's room, she'd forgotten why they'd been there in the first place.

"We have zero suspects," Nancy sighed as she, Bess, and George walked up Berry Lane. "With the ducky derby tomorrow morning, what are we going to do?"

Suddenly . . . *BEEP, BEEP!*

Nancy turned to see Hannah's car stopping at the curb.

"I thought that was you, girls," Hannah called out. "I'm on my way to Main Street, so how about a lift?"

"Don't you usually walk to Main Street, Hannah?" Nancy asked. "It's not far from our house."

"I'm delivering that box of used clothes to March of Time," Hannah explained. "It's too heavy to carry."

"You mean the box that was in the hall?" Nancy asked.

Hannah nodded. "Someone from the store was supposed to pick it up yesterday," she said.

"They usually ring the doorbell, but for some reason, they seem to have forgotten."

"Did you call the store?" Nancy asked.

"I called this morning," Hannah replied. "The owner told me they *did* pick up a box yesterday!"

"They did?" Nancy asked.

"That's what they said." Hannah chuckled. "I think someone got their boxes a bit confused."

Nancy stared at Hannah. The people at the store may have been confused—but to her, things were becoming clearer and clearer!

# Clue Crew—and
# YOU!

Can you help Nancy, Bess, and George figure out this feathery fiasco? Or read on to find out who plucked the ducks!

1. So far, Nancy, Bess, and George have ruled out Antonio, Dorothy, and Kinsley as suspects. Can you think of someone else who might have taken the box of rubber duckies? Write down your suspects on a piece of paper.

2. The March of Time store told Hannah they picked up a box of clothes, but Hannah's box was never picked up. Why could this be an important clue? Write down your thoughts.

3. Antonio, Dorothy, and Kinsley all had reasons for wanting the rubber ducks. Can you think of any reasons someone might want three hundred thirty-five rubber duckies? Let your imagination fly, and write down your answer.

# Chapter

10

## LUCKY DUCKS

"Nancy, what's up?" George asked.

"Your eyes are as big as Frisbees!" Bess exclaimed.

"Hannah said the store picked up a box, right?" Nancy said excitedly. "Maybe they picked up the wrong box!"

"The box of rubber duckies!" Bess gasped.

"Whoa!" George exclaimed.

"Rubber duckies?" Hannah asked. "Nancy,

does this have something to do with the box you asked me about?"

"I hope I can tell you soon," Nancy said. "In the meantime, we *will* come with you, thanks!"

The ride to Main Street was quick. A bell above the door chimed as Hannah and the girls filed into the March of Time thrift shop. Standing by a hat rack was a woman wearing sparkly cat-eye glasses. She finished hanging up an old-timey sunhat and turned to her new customers with a broad smile.

"Girls, this is Dulcie Yu, the owner of the store," Hannah said. "Dulcie, meet Nancy, Bess, and George!"

"Welcome, ladies," Dulcie said. "How would you like to see our vintage kids' section? I'll bet you never wore a poodle skirt or polka-dot pedal pusher pants!"

"Yes, please!" Bess said excitedly.

"Bess, we're not here for clothes," George reminded her. "We're here for ducks!"

"Ducks?" Dulcie asked.

"Yes, Ms. Yu," Nancy explained. "Would it be possible for us to see the box you picked up from our house?"

"As I told Hannah, a box was picked up yesterday. Stanley, who works here on Fridays, picked it up in his car."

"His car!" George repeated. "That must be the car Hannah heard outside."

"I did?" Hannah asked, still confused.

Dulcie pointed to a door next to the counter. "The box is in the back room. While I go through this new box with Hannah, why don't you go on in and take a look?"

Nancy, Bess, and George dashed through the door, then looked around the room. There were rows of boxes everywhere!

"How will we find ours?" Nancy asked.

"We don't have time to look through all of them to find the missing ducks!" Bess wailed. "What are we going to do?"

With a weary sigh, Bess plopped down on a big box.

*SQUEEEEEEEAK!*

"Bess, did you just squeak?" Nancy asked.

"I heard it too," George said.

"I don't squeak!" Bess insisted. She looked down at the box she was still sitting on and gasped. "Maybe . . . maybe . . . omigosh!" Bess jumped up, and Nancy and George ran over to help her. The girls tore off the tape, then lifted the flaps.

"Ducks!" George shouted, jumping up and down.

"Hundreds of rubber duckies!" Nancy was so excited, she threw her arms around her friends.

Bess gave one of the ducks a squeeze.

*SQUEEEEEEEAK!*

"They're the squeaky kind, too!"

"We found them, Clue Crew," Nancy said, grinning. "We finally found the missing rubber duckies."

The girls shared a high five just as Dulcie and Hannah entered the back room.

"Did you find what you were looking for, ladies?" Dulcie asked.

"Yes!" Nancy said, relieved to share why she'd been so secretive lately. "You see, instead of picking up the box of clothes, Stanley took this one from our doorstep."

Hannah peered into the box. "Rubber duckies? Why were they so important?"

"Mayor Strong asked us to number each duck for the derby tomorrow," Nancy explained. "We left the box on the doorstep while we went to get ice cream, and when we got back, it was gone."

Hannah shook her head slowly. "Nancy," she sighed. "Why didn't you simply tell me or your dad? We could have helped."

"You're right, Hannah. I should have told you and Daddy right away. It's just that—"

"It's just that you're the Clue Crew," Hannah interrupted with a small smile. "I get it."

"I do too," Dulcie said. "You can, of course, have your box back."

"Thanks, Ms. Yu," Nancy said. "Now we have to go, because we have three hundred and thirty-five rubber duckies to number by tomorrow morning."

"Three hundred and thirty-five ducks." Bess looked a little green.

"We're going to be up all night," George moaned.

"In that case," Nancy said, "may I suggest a sleepover?"

"I am soooo tired," George said the next morning.

"Me too." Bess yawned. "And soooo happy!"

Bess gave a quick little twirl before saying, "I'm also loving my new polka-dot pedal pusher pants from March of Time!"

Nancy tried not to yawn as she smiled at her sleepy friends. She too was tired, happy—and proud. Not only had the Clue Crew found the missing ducks, but they'd also numbered all three hundred and thirty-five of them!

After they delivered the ducks, joining the crowd to watch the race was super fun. So was cheering for the winner—ducky number three, which had been sold to Mr. Murphy, Henderson's dad!

"It was nice of Mr. Drippy—I mean Mr. Murphy—to give Henderson the free movie tickets," Nancy said as they watched the last of the ducks bob toward the finish line.

"All that ice cream and free movies, too!" George said.

"I guess the Henderson's lucky number is three," Bess remarked.

"Three is our lucky number too!" Nancy said.

"It is?" Bess looked confused.

"How?" George asked, appearing just as baffled as her cousin.

"Watch!" Nancy said. She took out the clue book, turned to a clean page, and wrote in big letters:

*NANCY + BESS + GEORGE =*
*BEST FRIENDS FOREVER!*

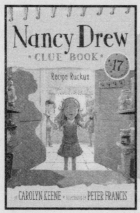

Test your detective skills with even more Clue Book mysteries:

Nancy Drew Clue Book #17: Recipe Ruckus

"Are you sure you feel okay, Nancy?" Bess asked. "If you have a fever, you should be in bed."

"I said I have *spring* fever," said Nancy with a smile. "That means I'm super excited for warmer weather, green trees, flowers—"

"Spring break," George Fayne cut in.

"Spring clothes," Bess said, striking a glam pose. "Like my brand-new spring jacket!"

Nancy and her two best friends were walking together up Main Street. It was the first week of spring break, so the usually busy street was busier than ever.

They had the same rules. They could walk up to five blocks from their houses as long as they were together. Since they were together most of the time, it was never a problem.

"Don't forget another awesome spring thing," Nancy said. "The River Heights Cherry Blossom Festival this Sunday."

"Who can forget with so many neat cherry blossom trees around?" Bess stopped to point at a tree sprouting fluffy pink buds.

"How did River Heights get so many of these trees in the first place?" George asked.

Nancy had just had this same conversation with her dad the day before, so she was happy to fill her friends in. "About a hundred years ago, the mayor of a Japanese town visited River Heights. He liked it here so much, he gave our mayor a gift of two dozen sakura."

"That's cool, I guess," George said, "but what about the cherry trees?"

Nancy giggled. "Sakura *are* cherry trees."

Bess scrunched her brow as she did the math.

"Two dozen equals twenty-four," she said. "That's a lot of cherry trees."

"And since they were gifts, that's a lot of wrapping paper," George joked.

The girls stood under the tree, catching the falling blossoms in their hands. They laughed as they gently blew them at each other.

"Speaking of gifts," Nancy said as they continued on their way, "that reminds me of my special mission today. I'm going to buy Hannah the perfect present for her birthday."

Hannah Gruen had been the Drews' housekeeper since Nancy was three years old. Like a mother, she made sure Nancy ate a good breakfast before school and did her homework after. Hannah also told the funniest jokes and baked the yummiest treats. Her birthday present had to be perfect. Just like Hannah!

"I have five dollars to spend on Hannah's present," Nancy said. "Any ideas?"

"How about five donuts from the Hole in One Donut Shop?" suggested George.

Nancy shook her head. "It's not a bad idea, but Hannah bakes even yummier donuts than the Hole in One."

"Then get Hannah something to use when she bakes," George said. "My mom uses tons of bowls for her catering business."

"Maybe."

Bess stomped her foot. "Maybe *not*! Instead of a boring bowl, how about a blouse or a scarf? New clothes are always a perfect gift."

"Or old clothes!" George said.

"*Old* clothes?" Nancy asked.

George pointed down the block. "The sign outside the March of Time thrift shop reads 'vintage clothes for old-timey prices.'"

The girls approached the store window, which displayed gently worn clothes from years ago. There were pastel-colored cardigans embroidered with pearls, sky-high platform shoes—even a beaded dress trimmed with fringe.

"We were in this store before," Nancy said. "When we worked on a mystery."

"When *aren't* we working on a mystery?" Bess asked, smiling. "We're the Clue Crew!"

Nancy, Bess, and George loved solving mysteries, and had their own detective club to prove it. They even had their own clue book where they wrote down all their suspects and clues.

"The owner of the store, Dulcie Wu, was a big help with our case," Nancy said. "Maybe she'll help me pick out a present for Hannah."

"We'll help too, Nancy," Bess said excitedly.

"*We* as in *me*?" George asked. She shook her head. "You know clothes aren't my thing."

"But *old* clothes are!" Bess said nodding down at George's holey jeans and scuffed sneakers. "Which makes you an expert."

Nancy giggled. Bess and George were cousins, but as different as day and night. Bess had blond hair, blue eyes, and loved new clothes and accessories. Dark-haired George loved accessories too, as long as they were for her tablet or computer.

"Okay, I'll help." George sighed. "But don't expect me to pick out anything pink or sparkly!"

When the girls entered the store, Dulcie was busy with a customer, so instead of being greeted by the owner, they were met by the musty smell of the vintage clothes hanging on racks and topping hat stands. Even the mannequins looked old-timey with their pencil-thin eyebrows and bright red lips.

"How about this for Hannah?" Nancy asked, pulling a floral blouse from a rack.

"Too frilly!" George said, shaking her head. She began sifting through the blouses herself, nixing them one by one. "Too stripe-y . . . too itchy . . ."

"What do you like, Bess?" Nancy asked. She turned to find Bess gazing into a mirror as she tried on accessories.

"I am soooo liking this super-cute hat! Have you ever seen a sunhat with a doll's head stuck on top?"

"Only in my nightmares!" George snapped. "Bess, take it off!"